The Fourth Floor Twins and the
Fortune Cookie Chase

Weekly Reader Books presents

The
Fourth Floor Twins
and the
Fortune Cookie Chase

DAVID A. ADLER
Illustrated by Irene Trivas

Viking Kestrel

This book is a presentation of Weekly Reader Books.
Weekly Reader Books offers book clubs for children from
preschool through high school.

For further information write to:
Weekly Reader Books
4343 Equity Drive
Columbus, Ohio 43228

VIKING KESTREL

Viking Penguin Inc., 40 West 23rd Street, New York, New York 10010, U.S.A.
Penguin Books Ltd, Harmondsworth, Middlesex, England
Penguin Books Australia Ltd, Ringwood, Victoria, Australia
Penguin Books Canada Limited, 2801 John Street, Markham, Ontario, Canada L3R 1B4
Penguin Books (N.Z.) Ltd, 182–190 Wairau Road, Auckland 10, New Zealand

First published in 1985 by Viking Penguin Inc.
Published simultaneously in Canada

Library of Congress Cataloging in Publication Data
Adler, David A.   The fourth floor twins and the fortune cookie chase.
(The Fourth floor twins series; #2)
Summary: Two sets of twins receive a message in a fortune cookie, warning them
to beware of a man in a blue hat.
1. Children's stories, American. [1. Twins—Fiction. 2. Mystery and detective
stories] I. Trivas, Irene, ill. II. Title. III. Series: Adler, David A.   Fourth floor
twins series; #2.
PZ7.A2615Fo 1985   [Fic]   84-21924   ISBN 0-670-80641-2

Printed in U.S.A. by The Book Press

To my good friends
Lenny and Ellen

CHAPTER ONE

"*Arf, arf, meow, moo, baa, baa.*"

It was a warm spring afternoon. Donna and Diane Shelton and their friends Gary and Kevin Young were walking home from school. Gary was making animal sounds.

"I'm going to be an animal doctor, a veterinarian," Gary told the others. "And sometimes sounds can calm an animal."

"I read a book about a zoo veterinarian,"

Kevin said. "He worked with lions, tigers, monkeys, and snakes."

The children walked into the lobby of their building. Max, the doorman, was there. He was on a ladder, changing a light bulb.

Gary barked.

"Out! Take that dog out," Max said. Then he looked down and saw Donna, Diane, Gary, and Kevin.

"Oh, it's my fourth floor twins," Max said

as he climbed down the ladder. "I have some real news to tell you."

Donna and Diane Shelton are identical twins. But they don't look exactly alike. Donna wears her hair in braids. Diane's hair hangs straight down. And Diane's front tooth is chipped. People notice it when she smiles.

Gary and Kevin Young are also twins. But they're not identical. Gary has curly brown hair and wears eyeglasses. Kevin has straight hair and freckles.

"Don't you want to know why Gary is barking?" Donna asked. "He wants to be an animal doctor."

"Baa. Baa."

Donna said, "Last week Gary wanted to be a comedian. And before that he was going to be a lawyer, a bank teller, and a plumber."

"Meow."

"When you hear what happened this morning," Max said, "you'll forget all about barking and meowing."

Max sat on one of the chairs in the lobby and said, "After you went to school, a little woman came into the building. She was pulling a shopping cart. 'Do you have any empty apartments?' she asked. 'Sure,' I said, and I told her about apartment 3C."

"Did you tell her about the faucet that doesn't turn off?" Donna asked.

"I told her."

"What about the window that rattles?" Gary asked.

"I'll fix all that. And anyway, she wasn't interested in faucets and windows. She wanted to see the oven. She turned it on. She took a thermometer from her shopping cart and put it in the oven. 'Good,' she said, when she took the thermometer out. 'I'll take the apartment.' "

"When is she moving in?" Diane asked.

"That's the *real* news. She moved in already. Two men, I think they're her sons, brought some furniture and boxes. One box

was filled with baking pans, flour, and sugar. I helped them carry everything into the apartment."

"Come on," Kevin said, as he walked toward the elevator. "Let's welcome her to the building."

Donna and Diane followed Kevin. Gary didn't.

"Did you ever think of getting some sheep as pets?" Gary asked Max. "They eat grass. You wouldn't have to mow the lawn. And you could sell their wool."

Max said, "I like to mow. Now hurry into the elevator before the doors close."

Gary ran into the elevator. He pushed the button for the third floor.

CHAPTER TWO

When the elevator doors opened, Donna ran out. "Here it is," she said, when she came to the end of the hall. "Here's apartment 3C."

Kevin knocked gently on the door and waited.

"No one is answering," Donna said. She put her ear against the door. "But she's in there. I can hear her moving."

Donna knocked hard on the door. Then she rang the bell.

"I'm coming. I'm coming," someone called from inside. The children saw an eye look at them through the peephole. Then a small, old woman opened the door.

"I'm sorry I didn't come right away, but I was putting some cookies into the oven. And look at my hands! Come in, children, while I wash this dough off."

Donna walked in first. The other children followed her into the living room. A couch, two chairs, and a small table were pushed into one corner of the room. In another corner were boxes, shopping bags, and a pile of clothing.

"I just moved in this afternoon," the woman said. "That's why this place is such a mess. My name is Mrs. Lee."

"We live upstairs, on the fourth floor. We came to welcome you to the building. I'm Kevin Young."

"I'm Donna Shelton."

"I'm her sister, Diane."

"And I'm Gary Young. Do you have any pets?"

The woman smiled and said, "No. I don't have pets. But I do have some cookies. I bake them for restaurants."

Mrs. Lee left the room again. When she came back, she was carrying a flat tin tray with rows of cookies on it. "You can each take one," Mrs. Lee said.

Donna quickly took a cookie from the middle of the tray. Then Kevin took one.

"Inside each cookie is a fortune," Mrs. Lee said.

"Maybe mine will say if I'm going to be a veterinarian," Gary said, as he took a cookie off the tray.

Diane reached for a cookie. Then she pulled her hand back. She reached for another cookie and changed her mind again. Then she closed her eyes and took one.

"Now, children," Mrs. Lee said, "I must get back to work. Why don't you visit me again after I've unpacked?"

When the twins were outside the apartment, Donna said, "Don't open your fortune cookies yet. Let's put our books away and then meet downstairs."

The twins rode the elevator to the fourth floor. Gary and Kevin walked down the hall to their apartment.

Donna and Diane live right next to the elevator. They opened the door to their apartment. Their older brother, Eric, was doing his homework at the dining-room table. His friend Cam Jansen was with him. Cam was writing with her eyes closed.

"Someone just moved into 3C," Donna said.

"Shh," Eric said. "We forgot our notebooks in school. Cam is writing down our math homework from memory."

The two girls put their books on the table

and then went outside and waited for the
elevator. It didn't come right away and they
ran down the stairs. They waited for Gary
and Kevin on the steps outside the apartment building.

"I think Diane should open her fortune
cookie first," Kevin said, as he walked outside. "She was the most careful picking it."

Diane looked up at Kevin. "Go on," he
said. "Break it open."

Diane bit into her cookie. A slip of paper fell out. Donna grabbed it.

"Look at this," she said, after she read the paper. Then she gave it to Gary.

"Beware of a man wearing a blue hat."

"Look!" Donna said. She pointed to a man on the opposite side of the street. He was walking toward the bus stop. The man was carrying a large briefcase. And he was wearing a blue hat.

CHAPTER THREE

" Let's follow him," Donna said. She stood and walked quickly toward the bus stop. Gary and Kevin ran after her.

"No," Diane said, but the others were too far ahead to hear her. Diane caught up with them at the corner.

"We can't follow him," she told Donna.

"Why not? We're not doing anything wrong. We're just walking."

The man was on the opposite side of the

street. He walked quickly. He walked past the bus stop. He stopped for only a moment at the corner. A car was coming, but the man didn't wait. He ran across the street, just ahead of the car.

"He's in a rush," Donna said. "He did something wrong and he's trying to escape."

The children waited at the corner. When they were sure no cars were coming, they crossed the street. The man was already halfway down the block. He turned and looked behind himself a few times as he walked.

Gary said, "He thinks he's being followed."

"Let's play tag," Kevin said. "We can run up and down the block and he won't know we're watching him."

Donna was "It" first. She ran down the block after the others. She reached out and touched Gary's shirt and called, "You're

It!'' Just as Gary began to chase Kevin, the man turned the corner.

The children looked up and down the street. No cars were coming. They quickly crossed. Now they were on the same side of the street as the man in the blue hat.

"We're making too much noise," Diane whispered. "Let's follow him quietly."

The children hid behind a large tree. They peeked out. They ran quietly to the next tree. They watched as the man switched his

briefcase from one hand to the other.

"Whatever he has in there is heavy," Kevin whispered.

There was a long row of hedges in front of an apartment building. The twins crouched and ran behind the hedges.

When the man reached the corner, he turned again. Then he put his briefcase down.

"I think he's a spy," Donna whispered. 'He's got some spy thing in that case. Those things are heavy. That's why he keeps

changing hands. And that's why he put it down. It's too heavy to carry for a long time."

The man bent down. He opened the briefcase and reached inside.

Donna whispered, "He's fixing that 'spy thing.' I'll bet it reads minds. He's not looking to see if he's being followed. He's looking for some important people, like generals and presidents. He wants to read their minds and find out their secrets."

The man closed the case and crossed the street. The twins saw him stop at a public telephone. The man put his briefcase down again. He took a few coins from his pocket and dialed.

"Did you see that?" Kevin asked.

"What?"

"Something inside his bag just moved."

CHAPTER FOUR

The man in the blue hat talked on the telephone for a while. The children watched as the sides of his briefcase continued to move. Then the man picked it up and walked farther down the block. He stopped at a small food store and went inside.

"Maybe there's another spy in that store. Maybe they're trading secrets," Donna whispered.

"And maybe he just went in to buy

some groceries," Diane said.

The door to the store opened. The man came out carrying his briefcase and a large shopping bag.

"Come on," Donna said. "Let's find out what he bought."

Donna and Diane went into the store. Gary and Kevin kept on following the man with the blue hat.

Donna went over to the woman behind the cash register. "That man who was just here, he told us to buy some more," Donna said.

"Some more what?"

"More of what he just bought."

"Aisle four," the woman said.

Donna and Diane walked down aisle four. The shelves on both sides of the aisle were lined with boxes, jars, and spray cans.

"That was dumb," Diane whispered. "You should have just asked her what the man bought."

"Spies don't work like that. They trick people into giving them information."

Donna and Diane looked at the shelves along aisle four. Diane picked up a box of plastic sandwich bags and said, "Maybe he bought these."

Donna shook her head.

Diane pointed to a large bag of dog food, a bag of kitty litter, and a family-sized package of lunch bags. But each time Diane pointed, Donna shook her head. They walked

past boxes of soap powder, bleach, dish-washing liquid, and floor wax. Then Donna stopped.

"This is it," she said, and picked up a can of insect spray. "He bought bug poison."

Donna ran to the front of the store. Diane followed her.

"Aren't you going to buy anything?" the woman behind the counter asked.

"No. I'm sorry," Diane said. Then she followed Donna out of the store.

Donna looked up and down the block. She didn't see Gary or Kevin. The two girls ran to the corner. Donna crossed the street. Diane turned the corner. After walking a few blocks and not finding either Gary or Kevin, the two girls met again in front of the food store. Gary was there, waiting for them.

"He bought poison," Donna said, "a whole lot of it."

Diane told Gary, "We really don't know what he bought."

"Come with me," Gary said. "Kevin is waiting for us."

Gary led Donna and Diane to a summer day camp near a busy road. There was a wire fence around the camp. They went through the front gate, which was open. They walked past empty yellow, green, red, and gray playhouses. Each house had shutters and was surrounded by a white picket fence.

"This is it," Gary said, when they came

to a small purple playhouse. "This is where
Kevin is waiting."

Gary and the girls looked for Kevin. They
walked around the house. Kevin was gone.

CHAPTER FIVE

Gary said, "He was right here when I left. He said he wouldn't move until I came back."

Gary turned. "Kevin and I saw the man go into a red barn. And now the barn is gone."

Diane gently patted Gary's shoulder and said, "A barn can't disappear. Now think. Where was Kevin and where was the barn?"

"Kevin was behind the purple house. And the purple house was near the red barn."

Donna pointed to the other side of the camp and said, "There's another purple house. Maybe that's where Kevin is waiting."

The children ran from one small building to the next until they came to the purple house. They quietly walked around to the back of the house. Kevin was waiting there, next to a pile of broken furniture.

"Someone else is in the barn with the

man," Kevin said. "I know because when he came to the door, he didn't open it. Someone opened it from the inside."

Donna whispered, "Maybe the door has an electronic eye. It looked at the man and knew that he was one of their spies. So it let him in."

"There are some windows along the side of the barn," Kevin said. "I'm going to look in. If something happens to me, you run and get help."

"Why don't we get help now? Why don't we call the police?" Diane asked.

Kevin said, "And what will we tell them? That a fortune cookie told us to beware of a man in a blue hat? That Donna thinks the man is a spy?"

Kevin walked quietly to the barn. He crawled beneath one of the windows. He stood up slowly and looked through the window for a while. Then he ran back to the others.

"He's not a spy. Maybe he's a veterinarian," Kevin said.

"If he's a veterinarian, why did he buy all that poison?" Gary asked.

"Listen. There's a woman in there. She must be the person who opened the door," Kevin said. "The room is filled with dogs and cats. And that big bag he bought was dog food."

"I'm going to look," Donna said. She walked quietly to the barn. Gary followed her.

"Why don't you go, too?" Kevin asked Diane. "I'll wait here. If anything happens, I'll run to the police."

Diane crawled to the barn. She stood between Donna and Gary and looked through the window.

"Look at that," Gary said. "Most people think dogs and cats can't get along. But they can."

Just then a small dog barked. It began

chasing one of the cats. A few of the other dogs barked and began chasing the cat, too. The man ran after the cat and picked it up.

"Why would they want so many pets?" Donna asked.

"Having a lot of pets is like having a lot of friends," Gary said.

"Look at the woman," Diane whispered. "Look what she's doing."

The woman was wearing a short skirt and T-shirt. The children watched as she tied on a few layers of padding. Then she put on a large dress covered with pictures of tiny flowers. The woman put on a gray wig and a pair of eyeglasses. She picked up a small white poodle and was about to leave the barn.

"Quick!" Donna said. "Let's get away from here."

The children ran to the purple house. Gary said, "They may not be spies, but they're up to something."

The barn door opened. The woman came out carrying the poodle.

"Who's that?" Kevin asked.

"That's the young woman with the short skirt. She's wearing a disguise," Donna said.

The woman walked past the front of the purple house. She was walking toward the gate.

"Come on," Donna said. "Let's follow her."

CHAPTER SIX

" I read about poodles. They're the smartest of all dogs. And they're very good swimmers," Gary whispered, as they followed the woman.

"Shh," Diane said.

The woman walked a few blocks to a large house. She rang the doorbell and waited. The twins watched as the door was opened and the woman went inside. A few minutes later she walked out. She was no longer carrying the poodle.

"Maybe the man in the blue hat and that woman are dog sitters. They take care of other people's dogs while the people are on vacation," Kevin said. "I read about some college kids who do that. It's a good way to make money."

"I think there's a veterinarian living in that house," Gary said. "The woman brought her dog in so he could get his shots."

Donna said, "I still think they're all spies. There's a secret spy code inside the dog's collar."

"Shh," Diane said. The woman was walking toward them. The twins were hiding behind a car. They waited quietly until the woman walked past.

"Now look!" Diane said.

She pointed to the front door of the house. A man was coming out. He was wearing a dark suit and necktie. And he was leading a small white poodle on a leash.

"I missed you, Daisy. I really did," the man told the dog. "Did you miss me?"

Donna walked out from behind the car. She quickly caught up with the man.

"That's a nice dog you have there," Donna said to the man.

"Yes. Daisy is a wonderful dog."

"You know, I saw a woman walk past just a few minutes ago. She was carrying a dog that looked just like your Daisy."

"That *was* Daisy. She was lost and that nice woman found her."

"Oh. Well, have a nice day," Donna said, and she ran back to the others.

"That dog was lost," Donna told Diane, Gary, and Kevin. "The woman with the wig found her. I'll bet she got a reward."

Kevin jumped up and said, "Let's get back to the camp. I think I know what those two are up to."

On their way to the camp, the children

saw the woman. She was reading the signs tacked on a tree. She pulled one sign down, folded it, and put it in her handbag.

At almost every corner there were trees and telephone poles with signs. The woman stopped at all of them. Whenever the woman stopped, the twins hid behind a car and watched her.

At one corner, when the woman reached to pull off a sign, her wig fell off. The woman picked up her wig and put it in her handbag.

Then she carefully folded the sign and put it in her handbag, too.

The woman walked through the gate and into the day camp. She went into the red barn. The twins hid behind the purple house. Donna took a broken bench from the pile of furniture and sat on it.

"I know what they're doing," Kevin whispered.

When Kevin whispered, Donna moved closer to hear. The legs on the bench bent.

"So do I," Diane said. "They're stealing people's pet dogs and cats. Then one of them puts on a disguise, returns the animal, and collects a reward."

Gary said, "That's terrible. Those poor animals."

"You know what I think," Donna whispered and leaned forward. The legs of the bench bent some more.

Suddenly the bench collapsed.

"Shh," Diane said.

There was another sound. A door had opened. Kevin peeked around the corner of the purple house and looked at the red barn. The man in the blue hat was standing by the open door. The man was looking right at Kevin.

CHAPTER SEVEN

" Let's run!" Kevin said. "He saw us."

Gary ran toward the gray house. The man ran after him. As the man chased Gary around the house, he bumped into Donna. She was looking for the front gate.

"Excuse me," the man said. Then he said, "Hey! What are you doing here?" And he began to chase Donna around the yellow house.

Diane ran past. "How did *you* get there?" the man asked.

"Over here! Over here!" Kevin called from the front gate. Diane and Gary ran toward him.

"Hey, stop!" the man called.

Just then Donna ran past him. The man reached out and caught her by the arm.

"But you just ran that way," the man said. Then he looked toward the gate and saw Diane. "So you're twins, are you? Well, what are you doing here?"

"This is a children's camp," Donna said, "and we're children."

"But it's not summer. Come with me."

"Help me load the car," the woman called.

The man led Donna back to the car and put her inside. Then he helped the woman carry the animals into the back of the car. He opened the door to put two dogs inside and a cat ran out. The man chased after the cat, but he had left the door open. Donna, two cats, and a dog ran out.

"Let's get out of here. That man is after us," Gary said, as he ran through the front gate.

"I'm staying," Diane said. "I'll try to help Donna."

"I'm staying, too," Kevin said.

"And I'll get the police," Gary said. He ran outside the camp. When he came to a traffic light, he saw a police car. Its lights were flashing. Behind it was a red sports car. The police officer was writing a ticket.

"You have to help us. You have to!" Gary told the police officer. "A man and a woman are chasing us. They're thieves. They steal cats and dogs."

"I think you should help the boy," the man in the sports car said. "That's more important than giving me a ticket."

"He can wait," the officer said, and he went on writing the ticket.

"But they're after us," Gary said.

Finally, the red car drove off. "Well now," the officer said. "What's your problem?"

Gary told him all about the fortune cookie, the briefcase, the animals, and the rewards.

"Well," the officer said. "Let's go to the camp."

Gary got into the police car. The two-way police radio was on. Gary heard reports of a car accident, a broken traffic light, and a call for help from a fruit store owner.

The officer picked up the radio phone, pressed a button, and spoke into it. "Car 358 to radio. Checking report of two dog- and cat-nappers holding out at the Adams Summer Day Camp."

When they drove into the camp, the officer laughed. The man and woman were running around the car and the red barn. Dogs and cats were running through their

legs and past them. Some were running in and out of the car and barn.

Kevin, Donna, and Diane were watching from behind the purple playhouse. "It was easy for me to get away," Donna told Gary and the police officer. "While the thieves were chasing the dogs and cats, I just ran here and hid."

The officer and the twins watched the man

in the blue hat and the woman chase after the stolen pets. Then the officer picked up his phone and spoke into it. "Please send a van and a second car to the Adams Camp."

After he hung up the phone, the officer told the twins, "I don't know what's going on here. But before I check into it, I want some help. There may be trouble."

A short while later, the van and police car came with sirens and flashing lights. The man and woman tried to escape, but there was no place for them to go. There was only one opening in the gate, and the police cars were parked right there.

The police caught the dogs and cats and placed them in the van. Many of the animals wore metal tags with their names and the names and addresses of their owners. Inside the barn the police found a whole pile of reward posters for lost dogs and cats.

When the police asked the man in the blue hat and the woman what they were doing, they didn't answer. But then one police officer rubbed his chin and wrinkled his nose. He looked angry.

"We stole the dogs and cats," the man said quickly. "We stole them. Then we returned them and got the rewards."

As they were led into the police car, the man asked, "How did you find us? No one knew we stole the animals. The owners thought they ran off."

"And they were always glad to pay the reward," the woman said.

Donna told the man, "We had a fortune cookie. It told us to beware of a man wearing a blue hat. That's why we followed you."

As the man and woman were led into a police car, the man pointed to the police. He said, "But they're wearing blue hats. You should have followed them and not me."

The police officers and the twins gathered the animals. After they put each one in the

van, they were careful to close the door.

One of the officers drove the twins back to their apartment building. He told the children that the police would return the animals to their owners.

CHAPTER EIGHT

"Where have you been?" Max asked, as the twins walked into the building.

"We caught two thieves," Donna began to say. But Max wasn't listening.

"So many things happened while you were gone," Max said. "You really shouldn't run off. You miss all the excitement.

"We had an oil delivery and the oil hose was leaking. Then I found a vegetable trail. That's right. I found a trail of tomatoes, peppers, radishes, and carrots in the lobby. I picked up the vegetables and followed the trail to Mrs. Wilson's apartment. There was a hole in her shopping bag."

Donna said, "Don't you want to hear what happened to us?"

"And Mr. Russell asked me to fix his TV," Max said. "He told me it broke during breakfast. 'Put the plug in,' I told him over the phone. That man doesn't remember anything. He pulls the TV plug out to plug in his toaster. Then he forgets what he did and thinks his TV is broken. It happens every time he makes toast."

"We caught two thieves," Donna said.

Ring. Ring.

Max picked up the lobby telephone. "Max here." He listened for a while. Then he said, "I'll be right up."

Max opened a closet door and took out a large tool bag. As he walked to the elevator, he said, "Come with me, twins. It's the woman in apartment 3C. She wants me to fix a broken faucet."

"That's Mrs. Lee," Kevin said.

As Donna walked into the elevator, she asked Max, "Don't you want to hear about the dogs and the cats and Mrs. Lee's fortune cookies?"

"Hey! I never opened my fortune cookie," Gary said. He reached into his pocket and took out pieces of a broken cookie. He reached in again and took out a slip of paper.

"*Beware of a man in a blue hat.* Mine is the same as Diane's."

Kevin pulled the fortune out of his cookie and read, "Beware of a man in a blue hat."

"Mine says the same thing," Donna said.

The door to 3C was open. Mrs. Lee was in the hall waiting for Max.

"Hey," Donna said, as she walked toward Mrs. Lee. "What's with these cookies? We all had the same fortunes."

Mrs. Lee laughed and said, "Let me show

Max the broken faucet. Then I'll tell you about the cookies."

Donna told Mrs. Lee, "Max knows which faucet is broken. It's the one he keeps fixing. It never works."

Everyone followed Max into the kitchen. He put his tool bag down and turned on the hot water faucet. There were banging and clinking sounds. But no water.

"I can't think up so many different fortunes," Mrs. Lee said, as she sat on one of the kitchen chairs.

"I bake trays of fortune cookies. Each tray has twenty-five cookies. And each cookie on a tray has the same fortune inside. I put the cookies in a bag, like these." She pointed to large plastic bags filled with cookies.

Max banged on the faucet with his fist. No water came out.

"But the fortunes in each bag are different. When someone in a resturaunt asks for a plate of cookies, the waiter takes one from each bag. That way he knows that each fortune on the plate will be different."

Max banged again on the faucet.

"That's very smart," Diane said.

Mrs. Lee smiled. "The fortune you had is one of my favorites. People have come back and said, 'I should have listened to my fortune. A man in a blue hat gave me a ticket.' You know, the police wear blue hats."

Max crawled beneath the sink. He took some tools from his bag and started working on the pipes.

"Other people wear blue hats, like thieves," Donna said. And she told Mrs. Lee about their adventure.

Max gripped one of the pipes with a wrench. He turned it, and water poured onto the kitchen floor. Max's face and shirt were soaked. Mrs. Lee ran to get some towels. Max quickly turned the pipe again and the water stopped.

As Mrs. Lee mopped up the water, she told Max, "I think I have the perfect fortune cookie for you."

She took a cookie from one of the plastic bags and gave it to Max.

"The fortune I gave the twins was a good one. It made them heroes. I think this one is just right for you."

Max broke open the cookie. He took out a slip of paper and read, "Today is a good day to seek some help."

Max said, "The cookie is right. I'll call a plumber."

"But beware if the plumber . . ." Donna said.

Then Diane, Gary, and Kevin joined Donna and said, "Beware if the plumber is a man in a blue hat!"